Owl has been out all night.
He has been very busy.
Owl is very tired. He goes
to sleep. Along comes Fox.
"Wake up, Owl," says Fox.
"I want to talk to you."
Owl wakes up.
He listens to Fox.

DRAGON AND SLEEPY OWL

BY
LUCY KINCAID

ILLUSTRATED BY
ERIC KINCAID

Brimax . Newmarket . England

Dragon lives in the wood.
He has many friends.
Owl is Dragon's friend.
Owl is on his way home.

Fox has gone. Owl is asleep. Along comes Rabbit.

"Wake up, Owl," says Rabbit. "I want to talk to you."

Owl wakes up.

He listens to Rabbit.

All the animals want to talk to Owl. Owl is very tired. He cannot work day and night.
He must get some sleep.
Owl goes to see Dragon.

"Will you stand under my tree?" says Owl. "Will you see that no one comes to talk to me? I must get some sleep."
"I will come now," says Dragon.
Owl goes back to his tree. Dragon stands under the tree.

A mouse comes to see Owl.
Dragon growls.
The mouse runs away.
A squirrel comes to see Owl.
Dragon growls.
The squirrel runs away.
Dragon growls when anyone comes near the tree.

"Are you asleep, Owl?"
says Dragon.
"No," says Owl.
"Why not?" says Dragon.
"Your growls keep me
awake," says Owl.
"I am sorry," says Dragon.
"What can I do?" says
Dragon.

The bees know what to do.
They know a sleeping
song.

"Hum Hum Hum," hum
the bees. "Close your eyes.
Go to sleep.

Hum Hum Hum."
Dragon hums too.

"Hum Hum Hum," hums
Dragon. "Close your eyes.
Go to sleep.

Hum Hum Hum."

Owl's eyes are shut.
Owl is asleep.
"Do not stop humming,"
say the birds. "Owl will
wake up if you do."
Dragon keeps on humming.
So do the bees.

HM-MM-MM-MM-MM

HM-MM-MM-MM-MM-MM-MM

HM-MM-MM-MM-MM-MM-MM-MM

The animals listen to the song. They get sleepy.
The birds listen to the song.
They get sleepy.
Soon they are all asleep.

The bees are awake.
The bees are still
humming.
Dragon is still awake.
Dragon is still humming.
The bees are getting
sleepy. Dragon puts his
paws over his ears.

The bees are asleep.
Dragon is still awake.
His paws are over his ears.
Dragon cannot hear the
sleeping song.

Owl wakes up.
"I cannot hear anyone,"
says Owl.
Dragon tells him they are
all asleep.
Owl laughs when he sees
them asleep. Owl laughs
so much that they all wake
up.
And then they all laugh
too.

Say these words again

busy	work
friends	night
listen	sleepy
eyes	sorry
talk	paws
tired	laugh
squirrel	growls